For Andy

First published 1991
by Walker Books Ltd, 87 Vauxhall Walk
London SE11 5HJ

© 1991 Anita Jeram

This edition published 1992
Reprinted 1992

Printed and bound in Hong Kong by
Sheck Wah Tong Printing Press Ltd

British Library Cataloguing in Publication Data
Jeram, Anita
It was Jake.
I. Title
823'.914 [J]
ISBN 0-7445-2310-9

# IT WAS JAKE!

## Anita Jeram

WALKER BOOKS
LONDON

Danny has a very special friend, his dog Jake.

Everywhere that Danny goes,

Jake goes too ...

and he can do almost as many things as Danny.

One day, Danny was at home.

"I'm bored," he said.

Then he had an idea.

"I know," Danny said to Jake,

"let's dress up!"

Later Danny's mum came in. "Oh, what a mess!" she cried,

when she saw the clothes on the floor.

"It wasn't me, Mum," said Danny.

" It was **Jake !** "

"When you've tidied up,"

said Danny's mum, "take Jake

outside, and make sure you

keep him out of mischief."

In the garden
Danny had
another idea.

"I know," he said,

"let's dig for buried treasure!"

So he did.

He dug near the flowers...

He dug under the tree...

He dug everywhere.

But he didn't find

any buried treasure.

After a while, Danny's mum came out to look for him.

"Oh, look at my flowers!" she gasped. "What have you done?"

"It wasn't me, Mum," said Danny.

" It was **Jake !** "

"Go and get cleaned up straightaway,"

she shouted. "And take that

wretched dog with you!"

In the bathroom

Danny said to Jake,

"If I have to have a wash,

I think you should

have one too."

But then Danny heard his mum coming.

"Mum…" said Danny.

"Look what Jake did!"

"Oh no!" said his mum.

"If that dog misbehaves

once more, there will

be trouble!"

"Come on Jake," Danny said. "Let's find something quiet to do."

Soon he was busy

cutting paper shapes.

"Now that's the last straw!" said Danny's mum

when she saw the paper everywhere.

"But it wasn't me, Mum," said Danny. " It was **Jake !** "

"Don't blame Jake!"

said his mum crossly.

"I think you must have made

all the mess because ...

but you

can go

to bed

without

any."

Because Danny really was sorry for being naughty

and for blaming everything on Jake, his mum brought him

a glass of milk and some toast anyway.

# MORE WALKER PAPERBACKS
## For You to Enjoy

### LITTLE RABBIT FOO FOO
by Michael Rosen / Arthur Robins

No one's safe when bully-boy biker bunny hits the forest! A new version of a popular playground rhyme by the author of the Smarties Book Prize Winner, *We're Going on a Bear Hunt.*

"Simple and hilarious… I laugh every time I think about it." *Susan Hill, The Sunday Times*
ISBN 0-7445-2065-7   £3.99

### JANET'S PONIES
by Kady MacDonald Denton

The delightful story of a girl's game of make-believe with her two younger siblings.

"Full of mischief and fun. The tongue-in-cheek humour will be appreciated by young children." *School Librarian*
ISBN 0-7445-2063-0   £2.99

### MORAG AND THE LAMB
by Joan Lingard / Patricia Casey

The farmer is concerned that Russell's dog Morag might worry the sheep – but she ends up saving a lamb!

"A delightful story with true to life illustrations." *Nursery World*
ISBN 0-7445-2030-4   £3.99

**Walker Paperbacks are available from most booksellers, or by post from Walker Books Ltd, PO Box 11, Falmouth, Cornwall TR10 9EN.**

To order, send:
Title, author, ISBN number and price for each book ordered, your full name and address and  a cheque or postal order for the total amount, plus postage and packing:

UK and BFPO Customers – £1.00 for first book, plus 50p for the second book and plus 30p for each additional book to a maximum charge of £3.00.
Overseas and Eire Customers – £2.00 for first book, plus £1.00 for the second book and plus 50p per copy for each additional book.
Prices are correct at time of going to press, but are subject to change without notice.